For Tess and her great-grandfather Albert Swerts
- An

For Herman Pieter Proppenschieter (grandpa)
- Jenny

First published in Belgium and Holland by Clavis Uitgeverij, Hasselt – Amsterdam, 2012
Copyright © 2012, Clavis Uitgeverij

English translation from the Dutch by Clavis Publishing Inc. New York
Copyright © 2013 for the English language edition: Clavis Publishing Inc. New York

Visit us on the web at www.clavisbooks.com

Get Well Soon, Grandpa! written by An Swerts and illustrated by Jenny Bakker
Original title: *Lieve opa, ik help je wel*
Translated from the Dutch by Clavis Publishing

ISBN 978-1-60537-155-9

This book was printed in April 2013 at Proost, Everdongenlaan 23, 2300 Turnhout, Belgium

First Edition
10 9 8 7 6 5 4 3 2 1

Get Well Soon, Grandpa!

An Swerts & Jenny Bakker

Clavis

NEW YORK

$\mathcal{F}$aye has packed her little suitcase. She's packed her pajamas, slippers, toothbrush, comb, and favorite cuddly bunny and she's ready to go. She's spending the night at Grandpa Bert's! Faye loves staying over at Grandpa Bert's house—they always have so much fun together.

"There is my sweet girl! So nice to have you here!" Grandpa Bert says cheerfully. "Do you feel like making pancakes?"
"Yum!" Faye beams. Together they get to work.
The flour flies, the sugar sprinkles, and an egg falls on the floor. *Splat!* But Grandpa Bert doesn't mind a little mess—just as long as the pancakes taste good!

After a pancake dinner, Faye and Grandpa Bert take Grandpa's dog Toby to the park. The sun is starting to set, making the leaves on the trees glow a beautiful orange.

When they get home, Grandpa Bert makes a cup of hot milk for Faye and they settle down into the rocking chair together. Grandpa Bert always reads Faye two bedtime stories: first a scary story and then a funny story. "That way, you'll have nice dreams," says Grandpa Bert. Faye doesn't know if that's true, but she always sleeps really well at Grandpa Bert's.

*F*aye wakes up to the delicious smell of frying bacon and eggs. "Good morning, sunshine!" Grandpa Bert calls as he bustles about the kitchen. He arranges two eggs and a slice of bacon on a plate so it looks like a happy face. "Always better…" Grandpa says, nodding at Faye. "…to eat a happy breakfast!" Faye shouts. They both laugh.

Grandpa Bert goes into the bathroom to shave. Faye sits on a small stool, meant just for her, to watch. *Shush, shush*—Grandpa Bert brushes a thick layer of white foam on his face. *Wick, wick*—Grandpa Bert carefully slides a small blade over the prickly stubbles until his skin is silky-smooth. And now comes Faye's favorite part— Grandpa Bert takes a beautiful glass bottle of aftershave from the cabinet, unscrews the cap, and lets Faye sniff. *Mmmm!* Delicious!
"Now we're ready for the day," Grandpa Bert declares. But something isn't right….

*S*uddenly, Grandpa Bert groans.
"Grandpa, are you okay?"
But without a word, Grandpa Bert
collapses and falls to the floor!
"Grandpa! Grandpa!" Faye shrieks.
He doesn't seem to hear her or see her.
What do I do? Faye wonders fearfully.
Then she remembers what she's
supposed to do in an emergency.
She picks up the phone and presses
the number one. That's the button that
makes Mommy's phone ring.

Very soon, Mommy arrives with
Grandpa Bert's doctor. Mommy looks
pale and her eyes are wet. She hugs
Faye to her, rocking her slowly back
and forth. Faye starts to cry.
"What's wrong with Grandpa Bert?"
"Oh, Faye, honey," she says, "that must
have been very scary for you to see
Grandpa fall. The doctor's going to
help him get better really soon, okay?"
Mommy's voice is shaking a little.

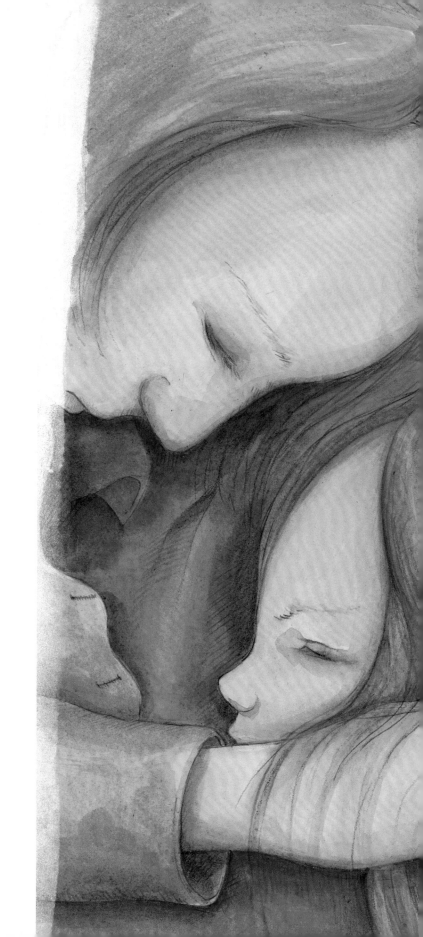

The doctor calls for an ambulance, which takes Grandpa Bert and the doctor to the hospital as fast as it can go. *Weeeeee-oooooo! Weeeeee-oooooo!* "We'll meet them at the hospital," Mommy explains. "Let's get in the car!" "Wait one sec," Faye says. She runs into Grandpa's bathroom and returns with the beautiful glass bottle of aftershave. "Can I bring this with me?" Mommy doesn't really understand, but she says, "Of course, honey. Now let's go."

$\mathcal{G}$randpa Bert has been in the hospital for several days. Finally, he is awake again, but he can't go home yet.

"Your grandpa had a stroke," the doctor says gently.

"A stroke?" Faye asks. "What's a stroke?"

"It's as if someone has had an accident in their head," the doctor explains.

"An accident—like with cars on the highway?" Faye asks.

"Well, a bit like with cars," the doctor says. "It's as if a car has stalled and tipped over in the middle of the road and no one can pass it."

"And that's why Grandpa can't do everything that well right now," Mommy adds. "He doesn't have much strength in his right arm and leg. Walking and picking up things is hard for him. Also talking and eating and drinking are hard because Grandpa's mouth is slowed down."

"Will he...will he be okay?" Faye whispers.

"The doctors don't know for sure," Mommy says.

"But, yes, they think he will be okay."

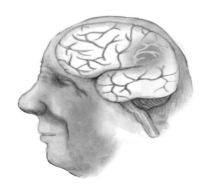

$\mathcal{G}$randpa Bert is in the hospital all summer long.
Faye visits him every night. She tells him what
she did that day: swimming with Sarah, playing
with Rickie, taking Toby to the park. When Faye
mentions Toby, Grandpa's eyes get a little wet.
Faye understands her grandpa misses Toby so much.

"Can I bring Toby to see Grandpa Bert some time?"
Faye asks the doctor one evening.
"Who's Toby?" the doctor wants to know.
"Grandpa's dog," Mommy explains with a smile.
The doctor shakes his head. "I'm sorry, but that's
against the rules. A hospital is no place for dogs."
Faye sighs. "I understand," she says.
But she really doesn't.

Back home, Faye wonders how she can bring Toby
to see Grandpa Bert. There *must* be a way!

The next morning it's bright and sunny.

"Can I take Toby for his walk?" Faye asks. Mommy looks up from her computer.

Toby's squirming and wagging his tail.

"Alright, then," Mommy says. "But don't go too far, Faye."

"We'll be back soon!"

Toby keeps stopping to sniff everything—like the hot dogs at a snack bar.

"Come on, boy, we're going a different way today," Faye says cheerfully,
giving his leash a little tug. Toby doesn't understand. They're going past places
he doesn't know—with all sorts of different smells.

Faye keeps walking. "Come on, Toby. We have to hurry!"

Faye and Toby come to a big,
tall building that has lots of windows.
Faye walks over to a tree by the
entrance, looks up, and starts to wave.
"Look up, Toby! Look up! There—
on the third floor, that's Grandpa Bert's
room! Grandpa! Grandpa!"
A familiar face appears in the window—
Grandpa Bert!
Toby wags his little tail super-fast and
starts barking loudly.
"Toby says hi, Grandpa!" Faye calls.
"Sorry we have to go so soon,
but I got to get back. 'Bye!
Get well soon, Grandpa!"
Grandpa Bert watches as Faye and Toby
start walking home. His face breaks into
a lopsided smile.

*S*ummer is over and Grandpa Bert is no longer in the hospital. He's staying at Faye's house now. The stalled traffic in his head is not entirely gone yet.

"Will you take Grandpa something to drink?" Mommy asks. Faye goes to Grandpa Bert's room. She hesitates before opening the door. She's always a little bit scared that something else bad is going to happen to Grandpa. She hugs her cuddly bunny and tries to think of something happy. Whenever she's scared, she knows Grandpa Bert can see it in her eyes and it makes him sad.

Grandpa Bert is resting in bed. When he sees Faye, he gives her a great big lopsided smile. "There…is…my…sweet…girl!"

Grandpa talks very slowly and it's not always very clear what he's saying. But Faye understands him most of the time. Mommy says that after a while, Grandpa's speech will get much better with help from Lena. Lena's a speech therapist who does talking exercises with Grandpa several times a week. Faye also does the exercises with Grandpa. When she comes home from school, they read to each other from an adventure book. They alternate reading a sentence. Some letters are hard for Grandpa Bert to pronounce, especially the *F* and the *V*. For Faye, the *R* is hard to pronounce. When they mispronounce words, they just laugh and try again.

"Hello, there!" Tom, Grandpa Bert's physical therapist has arrived. Grandpa's right leg doesn't want to go up right and it drags a bit when he walks. Tom does exercises with Grandpa to make the muscles in his right arm and leg strong again. During the sessions, Tom tells jokes. Faye doesn't always understand them, but Grandpa thinks Tom's funny. Sometimes Grandpa Bert gets laughing so hard, he has to stop to take a deep breath. It's fun when Tom is around and Faye often does her own exercises on a towel right next to Grandpa Bert's bed to keep him company.

"Early one morning, Grandpa Bert looks in the mirror and says to Faye, "I want…to…shave… I look…scruffy! Will you… help me?"

"Of course, Grandpa!"

He picks up an electric razor from the bedside table. *Rzzz! Rzzz!* Grandpa moves the razor over his face with his left hand. He can't use shaving cream and a razor blade anymore; he needs two strong hands for that and his right hand is still weak.

"Now…we're…ready…for…the day!" Grandpa Bert declares and he gives Faye a slow wink.

"Not yet, Grandpa." Faye takes the bottle of aftershave she kept for Grandpa Bert while he was in the hospital. She splashes some liquid in her hand and softly rubs it into Grandpa's smooth cheeks.

Mmmm!

Toby sticks his nose in the air…and sneezes.

"Toby likes the smell of hot dogs much better!"

Faye and Grandpa Bert laugh and laugh.